GHOST *and* MAX MONROE

CASE #2

THE MISSING ZUCCHINI

the GHOST and MAX MONROE

CASE #2

THE MISSING ZUCCHINI

WRITTEN BY **L.M. FALCONE**

ILLUSTRATIONS BY **KIM SMITH**

KIDS CAN PRESS

To young detectives everywhere

Text © 2015 L. M. Falcone
Illustrations © 2015 Kids Can Press

Kids Can Press gratefully acknowledges the financial support of the Government of Ontario, through the Ontario Media Development Corporation; the Ontario Arts Council; the Canada Council for the Arts; and the Government of Canada, through the CBF, for our publishing activity.

Published in Canada and the U.S. by Kids Can Press Ltd.
25 Dockside Drive, Toronto, ON M5A 0B5

Kids Can Press is a Corus Entertainment Inc. company

www.kidscanpress.com

Edited by Yasemin Uçar
Designed by Marie Bartholomew
Illustrations by Kim Smith
Chapter icon illustrations by Andrew Dupuis

Printed and bound in Malaysia in 6/2017 by Tien Wah Press (Pte.) Ltd.

CM 15 0 9 8 7 6 5 4 3 2 1
CM PA 15 0 9 8 7 6 5 4 3 2

Library and Archives Canada Cataloguing in Publication

Falcone, L. M. (Lucy M.), 1951–, author
    The ghost and Max Monroe. Case #2, The missing zucchini / written by L. M. Falcone ; illustrated by Kim Smith.

(The ghost and Max Monroe)
ISBN 978-1-77138-154-3 (bound)   ISBN 978-1-77138-018-8 (pbk.)

I. Smith, Kim, 1986–, illustrator II. Title. III. Title: Missing zucchini.

PS8561.A574G463 2015   jC813'.6   C2013-908317-0

CONTENTS

PROLOGUE

Max sat down beside his grandfather. "Your brother, Larry, is a *ghost?*"

"Yup."

"And he *haunts* the detective agency in the backyard?"

"Yup." Harry shot some whipped cream into his mouth. "Sometimes he hangs around the house. But mostly, he sits in the coach house, bawling his eyes out."

"I heard crying!"

"That'd be Larry. He likes to have a good cry around this time of day."

Max shook his head. "Crying ghosts … haunted detective agencies … I'll wake up any minute and everything will be normal."

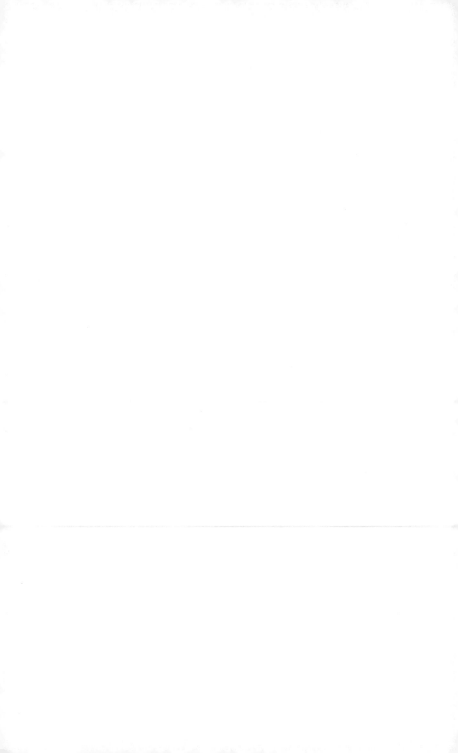

CHAPTER 1

THE BIGGEST POOP I'VE EVER SEEN

Max woke up to the sound of a train whistle. The sound made him think of traveling, and traveling made him think of his dad — a reporter who covered the news all over the world. Max's mom had died two years ago, and his dad's latest assignment had taken him to China, so Max was staying with his grandpa Harry and his great-uncle Larry in a big, old house in the country. Max slept in a room just down the hall from his grandpa.

And Uncle Larry? Well, who knew where he slept — or even *if* he slept — being a ghost and all. But if he did, it was probably in the old detective agency in the backyard.

Max rolled out of bed, pulled on his jeans and headed downstairs for breakfast.

Grandpa Harry was in the kitchen, lying in his hammock with a frog on his head.

"Why is there a frog on your head, Grandpa?" asked Max.

"His name's Fred, and he's helping me get rid of my headache. I don't believe in taking pills for every little thing."

Just then, Larry poked his head through the pane of the big bay window. His hand, on the other side of the window, held a filled pooper-scooper. "What the heck are you feeding that dog, Harry?"

"Puppy Chew. I had a coupon. Buy one — get one free."

"*Puppy* Chew?" said Larry. "This is the biggest poop I've ever *seen*. No way this mutt is a puppy. It doesn't take a detective to figure that out."

BUMBLING DETECTIVE

Back when Larry was alive, he was a detective. But he wasn't very good. His nickname was the Bumbling Detective because he never solved a case. Everything changed when Max came to stay with his grandpa Harry. After Max got used to the idea of living with a ghost, he and Larry became a successful detective team.

Max loved solving mysteries, and an invisible grown-up made a great partner.

Fred jumped off Harry's head and hopped away along the floor.

Harry sprang out of the hammock. "Where d'you think you're going?"

"He's behind the fridge!" shouted Larry, coming in through the window. "There he is! There he is!"

Harry crouched down. "Get back here, you little rascal."

Max left the frog hunting to his grandpa and Uncle Larry. He grabbed a bowl of cereal, walked out the back door and waded through the waist-high grass toward the run-down coach house where the Monroe Detective Agency office was. Instead of entering through the door, he climbed in through the window. The door key had been lost long ago.

ANSWER IT! ANSWER IT!

Max was just coming to the end of a *Starchy* comic when the phone rang.

"The phone! The phone!" shouted Larry, rushing into the office through the wall and waving his arms. "Answer it! Answer it!"

Max picked up the receiver of the old rotary phone. "Hello?"

Larry shifted excitedly from one foot to the other, like a kid who needed to pee.

"Max Monroe?" said the voice on the other end of the line.

"Yes," said Max, a little surprised that someone would be asking for *him* on the detective agency phone.

"This is Zeeta and Zelda Zamboni. We need your help. Our most prized possession has been stolen!"

Larry leaned in to listen. As he did, he caught sight of the *Starchy* comic on the desk. "Oh, oh, I *love* that *Starchy*!" he gushed. "It's the one where he has to save Chihuahuas that have landed on Pluto — the planet, not the dog. Then he gets —"

Max frowned at him, putting his finger

to his lips to try to shush him.

Larry nodded, then leaned back in to listen.

FOR CRYING OUT LOUD!

"We're friends of Marty the magician," said Zelda, "and he told us how you got him out of a sticky situation by finding Daisy Dee. He said you're a *great* detective. Will you help us? *Please?*"

Larry's eyes almost popped out of his head. "Say YES! YES!!"

Max didn't look too sure, so Larry grabbed the phone.

"Would you hold the line for one moment, please?" he said sweetly, then threw the phone into the desk drawer and slammed it shut.

"Max, don't you realize what a great *opportunity* this is? It's another chance to redeem the Monroe name — and another chance for you to be a detective. Kids your age have paper routes, for crying out loud! You've *got* to do it. For both of us."

Larry had a point — about the paper route, anyway. Max *was* enjoying being a detective. The summer was turning out way better than expected.

He opened the drawer and pulled out the phone.

"I'd be glad to help," Max told Zeeta and Zelda. "What's the prized possession that was stolen?"

"Our zucchini."

Max's face dropped. "Your *zucchini?*"

"Yes," said Zelda. "The one we're

entering in this year's Harvest Fair. This is the tenth year of the competition, and we've won nine years in a row."

"We're determined to make it ten!" Zeeta piped in.

Max slumped in his chair. "All right," he said. "Give me your address." Looking for a zucchini was sure to be duller than dirt — but he'd given his word, and he never went back on his word.

After Max hung up the phone, he turned to his uncle. "They want me to find their *zucchini*, Uncle Larry."

"So? Sherlock Holmes had lots of unusual cases."

Max shook his head. "I seriously doubt anyone ever asked him to find a missing vegetable."

CHAPTER 2

HOME OF THE WORLD'S LARGEST ZUCCHINI

Larry rushed to the garage to get the motorcycle. When he honked, Max slipped on his coat and met him in the driveway. Whenever Larry drove the motorcycle, he wore an aviator's cap, goggles and a long coat. Without them, he'd be invisible, and that would be a weird sight — a motorcycle with no driver. Grandpa Harry and Max were the only ones Uncle Larry let see and hear him.

Max put on his helmet and stepped into the sidecar.

Larry revved the engine a couple of times, then they took off like a flash.

When they reached the end of the block, Larry shouted, "Where are we going?"

Max looked at the crumpled paper in his hand and shouted back, "To 77 Hoodwinked Lane! In Harrow."

The motorcycle roared down the road. Half an hour later, Max and Larry passed a sign that said, *Welcome to Harrow (Home of the World's Largest Zucchini)*.

In the middle of a field stood a humongous zucchini made of metal.

Larry drove across the open field, then up a small hill, and turned onto a dirt road. They whooshed past farmers' fields with grazing horses and finally came to a neighborhood with wide, tree-lined streets. They found Hoodwinked Lane, turned left and, as usual, Larry screeched to a stop. They parked about a block away from Zeeta and Zelda's house so that Larry could stash his clothes in the sidecar.

When he was invisible again, he and Max headed toward number 77.

THE CASE BEGINS

All the houses they walked past had ordinary front yards with grass, trees and flowers. But one house, the one next door to the Zamboni sisters', was different. It had dozens of beautiful yellow rosebushes surrounded by a circle of red rosebushes. A man was standing out front watering the garden.

"Holy cow!" said Larry. "Those roses are big enough to swallow a cat."

Max spotted a name on the mailbox: *Leonard.*

"Beautiful roses, Mr. Leonard," he said.

Mr. Leonard released the handle on the hose nozzle, and the water shut off. "Thank you very much, young man. I take *great* pride in my garden."

Larry frowned. "Why's he wearing a fur hat on such a hot day?"

Max ignored the question. "I've never seen such huge roses," he said to Mr. Leonard.

Mr. Leonard beamed. "I grow vegetables, too — largest tomatoes this side of Toledo."

"I had an uncle who lived in Toledo," said Larry. "He never said anything about giant tomatoes. And he sure didn't wear a fur hat in the middle of summer."

Max hid his mouth with his hand and whispered, "It's his hair, Uncle Larry."

"Can't be!" Larry walked right through the rosebushes, leaned in close to peer at Mr. Leonard's head and even lifted some strands of hair.

"Uncle Larry!" hissed Max.

"Pardon?" asked Mr. Leonard.

"I … uh, I said, I'd love to see your tomatoes."

Mr. Leonard's face darkened. "Well, I don't *have* any this year," he said, almost snarling. "Thanks to *those* two next door."

"Zeeta and Zelda?"

"Around here we call them the Zucchini Sisters."

Larry smiled. "Zucchini Sisters? Has a nice ring to it." A truck slowly rolled by playing a jingle. "Ice cream!" shouted Larry, and he took off like a shot.

"What did the Zucchini Sisters do to your tomatoes, Mr. Leonard?" asked Max.

"I'll show you."

Mr. Leonard led Max into his backyard.

CHAPTER 3

HAVE YOU EVER SEEN SUCH PUNY TOMATOES?

Mr. Leonard's backyard was big and well kept. The lawn was mowed, the hedges were trimmed and there was a fountain in the middle.

"Take a look at that!" said Mr. Leonard, his voice cracking. He pointed to a garden full of scrawny plants with small, unripe tomatoes hanging off the branches. "They're all stunted!" he exclaimed. "Have you ever seen such puny tomatoes in all your life?"

Max nodded in agreement. "They are pretty small."

"My reputation will be ruined. I'll be the laughingstock of the community."

"How will the community know about your tomatoes?" asked Max.

"How will they *know*?!" Mr. Leonard's eyes practically bugged out of his head. "Because I'm the Tomato King, that's why! Every year I enter my tomatoes in the Harvest Fair Tomato Competition and, by golly, my tomatoes are winners. But there's no way that's going to happen this year — and it's all *their* fault." Mr. Leonard jabbed his finger toward Zeeta and Zelda's house.

"What did the Zucchini Sisters do?" asked Max.

"They grow their vegetables in different parts of their garden each year so the minerals in the soil don't get depleted. And *this* year they chose to grow their monstrosity of a zucchini right next to my fence! Why, its leaves grow ten feet high! And the shade extends halfway across my yard! Look for yourself." He waved his arms at the fence that separated his yard from theirs. Big green leaves crept over the top of the fence.

"Ten feet?" asked Max, looking at the leaves. By his estimate, they came up to about six feet at the most.

Mr. Leonard took another look. "That's strange. They were at *least* ten feet high yesterday morning. They completely blocked the sun!"

Larry appeared, holding a vanilla-chocolate twist ice-cream cone.

"What did I miss?"

Max's eyes opened wide. Just as Larry leaned in for a lick, Max slapped the cone out of his hand. It whizzed right behind Mr. Leonard's head and landed in some plants on the ground beside the fence.

"Hey!" said Larry, diving after it. "What did you do that for?"

Luckily, Mr. Leonard was too preoccupied with his problem to notice the flying ice cream. "My tomatoes haven't been able to get any sun all summer," he continued. "It's *impossible* to grow tomatoes without sun!"

Max noticed some three-leaf plants growing along the base of the fence. "That looks like poison ivy," he said, pointing to where Larry was crouched, trying to salvage what he could of his ice cream.

"Yikes!" Larry gasped and jumped back.

"You're very observant," said Mr. Leonard. "That's *exactly* what it is."

"It's growing through the fence into the Zucchini Sisters' yard," said Max.

"Good," sniffed Mr. Leonard. Then he

turned and stomped away.

"Let's go for more ice cream," said Larry.

"You can't just go running off, Uncle Larry. We have a mystery to solve."

"Oh, yeah. Sorry."

"And you can't go around *holding* things, either. It'll freak people out."

MY FINGER SLIPPED

When Max and Larry got back to the sidewalk in front of Mr. Leonard's house, Zeeta and Zelda were standing on the front porch of their big, green-shuttered house.

They waved at Mr. Leonard. "Yoo-hoo! Mr. Leonard! Hello!"

Mr. Leonard took one look at the sisters, grabbed his hose and sprayed them head to toe.

Max was shocked. Larry burst out laughing.

"Oops! Terribly sorry," said Mr. Leonard. "My finger slipped."

"Not to worry!" called Zelda, smiling. Even though they were dripping wet and their hair was hanging in their eyes, the sisters acted like nothing was wrong.

"Every time I see those two, I get so mad I could *spit*," muttered Mr. Leonard.

Larry pulled Max a few steps away and whispered, "Never stand too close to a man who might spit."

Max and Larry left Mr. Leonard to his watering and made their way toward the Zucchini Sisters' house. As they walked, Max took out his notebook and wrote …

Suspect #1 — Mr. Leonard

Motive — Revenge

"If Mr. Leonard stole the giant zucchini," said Max, "he could get revenge on the Zucchini Sisters for stunting his vegetables and ruining his gardening reputation."

"Right!" said Larry. "We have our first suspect."

CHAPTER 4

NO TIME TO DILLYDALLY

Max spoke with the two sisters on their front porch. Larry slumped down on a rocking chair and put his feet up next to a large potted plant.

"I'm just going to nip inside and get us some freshly squeezed lemonade," said Zelda.

"Thanks," said Larry. "I'm parched."

As Zelda stepped inside to get the lemonade, Zeeta motioned for Max to sit down, and she started to explain. "Every year, a vegetable competition is held on the last day of the Harrow Harvest Fair. My sister and I always enter the vegetable competition because, well, we grow unusually large zucchini!"

Zelda stepped back onto the porch holding a tray with a pitcher of lemonade and some glasses. "We *certainly* do," she said proudly. "And since the fair ends tomorrow, there's no time to dillydally." She set the tray down and popped straws into each of the glasses.

Zelda poured the drinks, and Zeeta continued. "As usual, everything was going just lickety-poo."

Larry giggled. "Lickety-poo. Write that down, Max. I want to remember that."

Max cleared his throat, hoping Larry would take it as a signal to be quiet.

"In fact, this year's zucchini was the largest we've *ever* grown. It weighed at least two hundred pounds."

"I had no idea a zucchini could grow that big," said Max.

"They don't," said Zeeta. "Ours is a freak of nature."

"At two hundred pounds," said Max, "your zucchini would almost certainly win the blue ribbon, wouldn't it?"

"You betcha," answered Zelda, as she

handed Max a glass of lemonade.

"My Uncle Louie," said Larry, "the one I told you about from Toledo? He once grew a twenty-pound potato. Then he had it bronzed."

Larry leaned over and drank through the straw in Max's glass. The lemonade disappeared. The sisters and Max stared wide-eyed at the glass.

"Your lemonade!" the sisters exclaimed at the same time, pointing at the empty glass.

Max gulped. He looked at Larry for help. "Umm ..."

Larry gave a satisfied sigh. "Ahh ... that hit the spot."

"The glass must have a crack in it," said Zelda.

Everyone looked down. There were puddles of water where the sisters had dripped after being sprayed by Mr. Leonard.

"Of course," said Zeeta. "Pour Max another glass, dear."

Zelda held another glass up to the light and examined it, then poured more lemonade.

OUR ZUCCHINI LOVED PUCCINI

"Ask the sisters how they grew a freaky two-hundred-pound zucchini," said Larry.

"What's the secret to growing such a big zucchini?" asked Max.

Zeeta and Zelda looked at each other and smiled.

"Now, promise you won't tell anyone," said Zeeta.

"I promise," said Max.

Zeeta looked around to make sure Mr. Leonard couldn't hear, then whispered, "Our secret is *music*."

"Music?" asked Max.

Zelda nodded. "We discovered early on that our zucchini *loved* Puccini."

"Puccini, the composer?" asked Larry.

"Puccini, the composer?" asked Max. (He'd never heard of him.)

Zelda grinned. "The one and only. From the time our zucchini was a little sprout, we put speakers on either side, and every day we'd play Puccini. The more music we played, the bigger it grew!"

"That's amazing," said Max.

Zeeta sighed. "It won't mean anything if we don't get our zucchini back before the competition tomorrow."

A REAL PEACH

"When did you discover it was missing?" asked Max.

"It was right after we got back from the Harvest Parade," said Zelda.

"We have a lovely parade on Main Street every year on the first day of the fair. *Everybody* goes," Zeeta explained.

"Everybody?"

"Yes, we're very proud of our parade."

"How long does it last?" asked Max.

"Oh, about an hour, wouldn't you say, Zelda, dear?"

Zelda nodded.

"That would give someone plenty of time to steal the zucchini," said Max, "without worrying about being seen."

Zelda shook her head. "We just can't

imagine *anyone* in our town stealing our zucchini. Everyone is so nice!"

Larry burst out laughing. "Yeah, that Mr. Leonard is a real peach."

"Do you know if anyone else around here is entering the zucchini competition?" asked Max.

"Well, there's Mr. Jordan," said Zeeta. "He lives in the big house at the end of the street."

"He grows some large zucchini that he enters in the competition every year," added Zelda, "and always does very well. He's come in second — how many times has it been now, Zeeta?"

"Well, not counting the year he was on vacation, I believe it's eight."

"He wasn't on vacation that year,"

corrected Zelda. "He was busy building the community center." She turned to Max. "It's named after him, as are many things in our town."

Max got up and said goodbye to the sisters. Once he was out of earshot, he turned to his uncle. "Let's pay Mr. Jordan a visit."

CHAPTER 5

GIANT BARBECUED CHICKEN LEG

When Max and Larry got to the end of the street, they found themselves in front of a gigantic house with stone lions on either side of the entrance.

"Whoa! This Jordan guy must be rich," said Larry. "I'll be back in a minute." Then he disappeared.

Max looked around. "Uncle *Larry?*"

Larry was nowhere to be seen, so Max walked alone up the long, winding driveway, climbed the front steps and rang the bell. Within seconds, an elderly gentleman wearing a black vest and tie answered the door.

"Are you Mr. Jordan?" asked Max.

"I'm Hemsley, Mr. Jordan's butler. May I help you?"

Larry appeared out of nowhere behind Hemsley. He was taking a bite out of a giant barbecued chicken leg.

"Want some chicken, Max?" offered Larry with his mouth full.

Max tried not to look at his uncle — or the chicken.

"We'd like to speak to Mr. Jordan, please," he said to Hemsley.

Hemsley tilted his head and looked around Max. "We …?"

"Um, I … *I'd* like to speak to Mr. Jordan, please."

"If you're selling something —"

"I'd just like to ask him a question."

One of Hemsley's eyebrows went up. "Very well. Come in."

YOU COULD BOWL IN HERE

Max stepped into the huge foyer. A grand staircase went up to the second floor, and a sparkling chandelier hung down from the ceiling.

"Get rid of the chicken," Max hissed at Larry.

"You could bowl in here," Larry said, making sure he kept the chicken leg out of sight behind the butler.

"This way, please," said Hemsley, leading them through a living room. Max noticed lots of paintings hanging on the walls, a grand piano in the corner and a fireplace with a fancy carved mantle.

Next they went through a dining room. The table seated fourteen people and had a big vase filled with fresh flowers on it. At the end of the room, there was an aquarium with colorful fish swimming around. Hemsley opened a patio door and waved Max outside. "Please have a seat. Mr. Jordan will be arriving momentarily."

"The *chicken*, Uncle Larry!"

"Okay, okay!" Larry snuck one last bite, then threw the chicken leg into the aquarium. As Max walked outside, Larry bent down and looked at the scattering fish. "Sorry, fishies, didn't mean to scare you," he said, before joining Max.

Max and Larry sat down at a table on the patio and waited.

"Look at the size of this yard, Max. It's like a golf course."

Max looked out over the grass. It seemed to go on forever. He noticed a garden off to the left filled with tall sunflowers. "There's no vegetable garden out here, Uncle Larry."

"I'm pretty sure this guy can afford to buy his vegetables at the supermarket."

"Yes, but where are his zucchini? Zeeta and Zelda said he enters one in the competition every year."

"That's right! Maybe he buys them from somewhere else and then enters them in the competition under *his* name! With his money, he could have them shipped from anywhere in the world!"

"That's a good point, Uncle Larry."

Whomp-whomp-whomp ...

Larry looked around. "What the heck is —?"

Whomp-whomp-whomp-whomp ...

The sound got louder and louder, and then a helicopter crested over some trees and flew in the direction of the house. It created a strong wind as it circled and came in for a landing on the lawn.

"Would you look at *that* — he has his own chopper!" said Larry. "I always wanted to take flying lessons. And then I died. Now I can fly anywhere I want!"

A tall, thin man stepped down from the

helicopter. He held a cane in his left hand and limped across the yard.

As the helicopter lifted off again, the leaves and branches of nearby trees whipped and swayed in the wind created by its blades.

HOW RUDE

"Who are *you?*" snapped Mr. Jordan.

Larry frowned. "What's got his knickers in a twist?"

"I'm Max Monroe, and I've been asked to help find Zeeta and Zelda Zamboni's stolen zucchini."

"I know nothing about a stolen zucchini," said Mr. Jordan, resting his cane against the table.

"Have you seen anyone suspicious hanging around the neighborhood?" asked Max.

"No, I haven't."

"Have you heard any unusual sounds?"

"Afraid not."

"Do you have any idea who might want

to steal the sisters' zucchini?"

"Haven't got a clue."

Larry leaned in. "He's a hard nut to crack, but don't give up, Max. Keep asking questions."

Max didn't get to ask any more questions because just then Mr. Jordan picked up a small silver bell from the table and rang it.

"Is he ringing for lunch?" asked Larry hopefully.

"Now, if you'll excuse me," said Mr. Jordan.

The patio doors opened, and Hemsley appeared.

"You rang, sir?"

"Please see this young man out."

"But I still have a few —"

Mr. Jordan cut Max off. "I have a splitting headache, and I need to get out of the sun."

He turned and limped into the house. Just as he reached the patio doors, Max called after him, "Put a frog on your head. It'll take care of that headache."

Mr. Jordan stopped but didn't turn around. "That's disgusting," he said and went inside.

"Did he just call Fred disgusting?" asked Larry.

"I guess so," said Max.

"How rude."

BEWARE OF DOG

Hemsley turned to Max. "Come this way, please."

Max, Larry and the butler went down some marble steps. As they walked along the stone path, Max noticed a fence at the side of the house, behind a high row of bushes. It had barbed wire running along the top. As he ran his eyes along the length of the fence, he saw a sign that said, *BEWARE OF DOG*.

Max caught up to Hemsley. "What kind of dog does Mr. Jordan have?" he asked.

"Mr. Jordan doesn't have a dog. Too many germs."

As they continued on the stone path, Max said, "I was just visiting the neighbors Zeeta and Zelda Zamboni."

"And how are the sisters doing today?"

"They're a little damp," Larry said, laughing.

"Their zucchini was stolen," said Max.

Hemsley looked surprised. "The one they're entering in the Harvest Fair?"

"Yes."

"I'm sorry to hear that."

"Yeah, I bet you are," muttered Larry. "What did you do with the freaky zucchini? Come clean, and we'll go easy on you."

Max glowered at Larry, then turned back to Hemsley. "The sisters mentioned that Mr. Jordan grows some pretty big zucchini."

"Never big enough to beat theirs, but *this* year might be different."

"Different how?"

"Mr. Jordan has hired the most highly regarded specialists to analyze his soil and recommend the best fertilizers. They're working around the clock so that at least *one* of his zucchini will be awarded the blue ribbon. This year, Mr. Jordan is determined to go home a winner."

WHAT SIGN?

After leaving Max at the front of the house, Hemsley went back inside.

"Why would a man who doesn't own a dog have a *Beware of Dog* sign?" said Max.

"What sign?" asked Larry.

"And why does his fence have barbed wire on it?"

"What fence?"

Max stopped and looked at his uncle. "How could you miss it?"

"Miss what?"

"Mr. Jordan's hiding something," said Max. "And I want to check it out."

"You're right. He's definitely hiding something. Yes, definitely … But where?"

"Behind the fence!"

"The fence! Of *course*!"

Max slipped behind some bushes and headed toward the side of the house.

CHAPTER 6

CAUGHT

Max continued to the fence. It was at least twice his height. He looked around for something to stand on and spotted a large green garbage bin with wheels. After pushing it up to the fence, he struggled to climb on top without tipping it over.

Larry floated effortlessly up in the air.

"Show-off," said Max.

Larry grinned. "Just one of the perks of being dead."

Max carefully got himself up on his
tiptoes and looked through the barbed wire.

On the other side of the fence was a
huge vegetable garden with a dozen
rows of very large zucchini. A man and
a woman, dressed in white lab coats,
stood at the far end. One was inspecting
the vegetables; the other was checking a
thermometer.

"Do any of those zucchini look like they might weigh two hundred pounds?" whispered Max.

"Not even close."

"Okay. Let's go."

Larry looked around. "Great view from up here."

As Max turned to jump down, Larry suddenly shouted, "Wait!"

"Why?"

"I can see right into Mr. Jordan's bedroom! The butler just came in carrying a silver tray with a glass of water on it. There's something else on the tray, but I can't make out what it is."

"It's not important, Uncle Larry. Come on."

"Wait! Wait! Wait!"

"*What?*" Max strained to get a better look

but couldn't get high enough.

"They're gloves! That thing I couldn't make out was a plastic bag with a pair of white gloves inside! The butler just snipped open the bag, and now Jordan's putting them on! Now he's reaching for the glass of water! Now he's popping a pill! Now … Uh-oh."

"What's wrong?"

"The butler spotted you!"

As Max spun around, his coat collar caught on the barbed wire.

YOU'RE CHOKING ME!

"Jump down!" shouted Larry. "And *run*!"

"*I can't!* My coat's caught!"

"Hurry, hurry!" urged Larry.

"Help me!"

"Okay, okay …"

Larry tried to untangle Max's coat, but the more he tried, the worse it got. He became hysterical. "It's no use! Ohmigosh! Ohmigosh! What are we gonna do?" Larry started bawling. "I shouldn't have been so nosy! I'm the worst detective ever! *IT'S ALL MY FAULT!*"

Larry kept yanking at the coat and crying, "Mr. Jordan's gonna have us arrested! And sent to the big house!"

"You're choking me!" cried Max.

"What are we gonna *dooooo*?!"

"Uncle Larry, let go!"

A ladder slammed up against the fence. Both Larry and Max gasped and turned to see Hemsley climbing up.

NO HARM DONE

"Now, just relax, young man," said Hemsley. He reached over and untangled the coat from the barbed wire. "There. No harm done."

Max jumped to the ground. Larry heaved a sigh of relief and floated down beside him. The butler climbed down the ladder.

"Thank you," said Max.

"Glad to be of service. Now, I suggest you get on your way before Mr. Jordan sees you."

"May I ask one question before I go?" said Max.

"What is it?"

"Why does Mr. Jordan wear gloves?"

"Mr. Jordan is a germaphobe. He never touches anything without his gloves. Now, off you go. He'll be coming out any minute to check on his zucchini."

Max and Larry quickly made their way out to the street and headed back toward the Zucchini Sisters' house. As they walked, Max took out his notebook and wrote …

Suspect #2 — Mr. Jordan

Motive — Wants to win

"If Mr. Jordan stole Zeeta and Zelda's zucchini and entered it as his own, he'd win the blue ribbon for sure," said Max.

"Right!" said Larry. "And it would finally put an end to his losing streak."

CHAPTER 7

IT'S MAKING ME HUNGRY

As Max and Larry neared the Zucchini Sisters' house, a delicious smell wafted through the air.

"What *is* that heavenly smell?" Larry asked.

"I don't know," said Max. "But it's making me hungry."

Larry followed his nose, floating from house to house, until suddenly he shot like a torpedo into the backyard of a house on the corner. "Over here, Max!"

Max followed the sound of Larry's voice and found him watching a sweet-faced lady placing bread pans out to cool on the deck.

"Ask her what she's baking," said Larry.

"Excuse me," said Max. "Can I ask what you're baking? It smells terrific."

The lady blushed and smiled. "It's chocolate zucchini bread," she said. "I've just baked five loaves. If you'd like to try some, I could spare a slice."

Max's eyebrows went up at the mention of the word *zucchini*.

I CAN'T BELIEVE IT'S ZUCCHINI!

Larry poked him. "Say yes! Yes!"

"I'd love some — thanks," said Max.

The lady scooted back into her house. A minute later, the door swung open, and she stepped out balancing a plate on her outstretched hands. Both hands were still in the oven mitts.

"I'm Edwena Whacker."

"Max Monroe."

Edwena held out the plate of chocolate zucchini bread slices. "Help yourself, Max."

Max took a slice, and then Edwena put the plate down on a small wooden table with a plant on it. When she turned her head, Larry swiped a slice and practically inhaled it.

"Oh … oh … oh …" he moaned.

"What's wrong?" asked Max, without thinking. He was worried that Larry was in pain.

"Wrong! Is something wrong?!" Edwena's face clouded over.

"This is the *best* bread I've ever tasted in my whole life!" raved Larry. "Tell her! Tell her!"

Max quickly took a bite. "Um … no, nothing's wrong. This is really, *really* good."

"I can't *believe* it's zucchini!" continued Larry.

"Hard to believe it's zucchini," said Max.

"I always liked zucchini, but I love this! I *love* it!" said Larry.

Max took another bite. It did taste great.

"Tell her! Tell her!" insisted Larry.

Max swallowed quickly. "It's really delicious, Ms. Whacker."

Edwena put both mitt-covered hands against her cheeks and grinned so wide her eyes disappeared. "Thank you. Thank you so much! It means a lot to me to hear you say that. A big bakery that sells to *all* the grocery stores is sending over three tasters this afternoon. If they like my zucchini bread, they'll give me a contract and a *huge* order. I really need that contract, but I've been worried sick my recipe won't be good enough."

Larry snuck another piece off the plate. "Good enough? It's great!"

"I think you have a winning recipe," said Max. "Those tasters will love this."

Edwena grabbed Max and gave him a bear hug. "You've made me so happy I could cry!" And then she did.

Max and Larry looked at each other.

IS SOMETHING WRONG WITH YOUR HANDS?

"Max, would you be kind enough to take a tissue out of my pocket?" asked Edwena.

"Um … sure." Max reached into Edwena's apron pocket and pulled out a tissue. Without taking off her oven mitts, Edwena took it and patted her eyes.

"Is something wrong with your hands?" asked Max.

"When I get nervous, I break out in hives." Edwena patted her eyes some more. "I put lotion on my hands this morning, and then put on these oven mitts. I don't want the tasters to see hives when they're tasting my zucchini bread. It might turn them off."

"I'm sure nothing will turn them off

when they taste this," said Max.

"You're too kind." Edwena blew her nose loudly.

"I hear there was a parade in town yesterday," said Max. "Were you able to go to it?"

"Usually I go with my neighbors Zeeta and Zelda," said Edwena, "but it just wasn't possible this year. I was much too busy baking and testing out different recipes. I had to get it just right. I *really* need that contract."

A loud horn made Max jump. A small moving truck drove up to the side door, and two large men stepped out. Edwena smiled. "Oh, wonderful!" she said. "My oven has arrived."

"How do you bake without an oven?" asked Larry.

"You don't have an oven?" asked Max.

"Yes, I do, of course. But I'm going to need more than one if I get that contract. And since this one was on sale, I took a chance and grabbed it."

The two men walked up to Max and Edwena.

"Max, these are my brothers, Eddy and Neddy. They're a great help whenever I need anything big moved."

Max shook hands with Eddy and Neddy. Then he told Edwena he had to get going. He thanked her for the zucchini bread and wished her good luck with the tasters.

When they were out of Edwena's sight,

Max said, "Suspect number three."

Larry's face fell. "You can't believe *Edwena* stole the zucchini! Why, she's sweeter than honey!"

"I know, Uncle Larry, but she's *desperate* to get that contract from the bakery. And you heard her — if she does get the contract, she's going to need a heck of a lot of zucchini to fill it."

Larry's shoulders sagged.

"And —" said Max.

"There's *more?*"

"Maybe those oven mitts Edwena's wearing aren't covering hives. Maybe they're covering a different kind of rash — like poison ivy? If she's the one who stole the zucchini, she might have touched the poison ivy when she was near the Zucchini Sisters' fence."

"No, no, no. They're *hives*. I'm sure of it."

"And —"

Larry covered his ears. "La la la la la," he sang. "I can't hear you. La la la."

Max shook his head, opened his notebook and wrote …

Suspect #3 — Edwena Whacker

Motive — Needs bakery contract

CHAPTER 8

I DON'T LEAVE FINGERPRINTS

When Max and Larry got to the Zucchini Sisters' house, they walked along the stone path that led to the side gate. Larry reached out to press the latch.

"Don't!" said Max.

Larry yanked his hand away. "What's wrong?"

"Fingerprints."

"I don't leave fingerprints."

"Oh, yeah, I forgot," said Max. "But other people do." He leaned in to inspect the metal latch. "This latch has a smooth surface."

Larry leaned in, too. "That's true. And a smooth surface means …?"

"It means that the oil from a person's fingertips will leave a print behind."

"Correcto!" Larry grinned. "Let's go buy some fingerprint powder."

"I think we can improvise," said Max. "Back in a minute."

WHAT DO YOU SEE, MAX?

Max knocked on the front door. When Zeeta and Zelda answered, he asked if they had baking powder, a soft-bristled brush and transparent tape. The sisters found the items and handed them over to Max.

Back at the gate, Max dipped the

paintbrush into the baking powder and lightly ran the bristles over the latch in short, quick strokes. Then he tore off some pieces of clear tape and pressed the sticky strips onto the metal. After carefully lifting each piece, he held them up to the sun and inspected them.

Larry looked excited. "What do you see, Max?"

"It's what I *don't* see, Uncle Larry."

"Huh?"

"There's not one single print."

"Maybe it's not the only way in?" suggested Larry.

"That's possible," said Max. "Or, maybe they wore gloves."

Max unlocked the gate and swung it open.

HE FLUNG A COW!

Once inside the Zucchini Sisters' backyard, Max scanned the surroundings. A fence went all around the property.

"I can't see any way someone could have gotten into this yard except through the gate," said Max.

"Unless they climbed over?"

"It's possible they could have climbed over to get *in*. But there's no way they could have climbed back *out* carrying a two-hundred-pound zucchini."

"They might have had a catapult and flung it over! In one of the *Starchy* comics, he flung a cow!"

Max's forehead furled. "Let's keep thinking. Okay?"

"Okay."

Max and Larry went farther into the large yard and headed toward the garden. As they walked along the grass, Max looked carefully at the ground.

"Looking for footprints?" asked his uncle.

"There could be some, but they're too hard to see on the grass."

DO YOU THINK THEY COULD MEAN SOMETHING?

"Wait a second," said Max, stopping and crouching down.

He started crawling along the ground in a straight line, pushing apart the blades of grass as he went. "Look, Uncle Larry."

"Look at what, Max?"

"These holes."

Larry crouched down. "They're awfully

small. Do you think they could mean something?"

Max frowned at his uncle. "Of course they could mean something."

Larry's eyes brightened, and he stood up. "Of course!" He leaned in closer to Max. "What do you think they could mean?"

Max stood up and focused on the grass. He measured the distance between the holes by putting one foot directly in front of the other, heel to toe. He counted, "One, two, three, four. One, two, three, four. They're all the same distance apart, Uncle Larry."

A POGO STICK!

Larry scratched his head. "What could make holes in the ground in such a straight line?" He moved along the grass from hole to hole. Then he swung around. "I've got it! A pogo stick!"

"*Who* would come into the yard on a *pogo* stick, Uncle Larry?"

"Someone from the parade?"

"The parade was downtown."

"You can move pretty fast on a — AHHHHH!!!!!!" Larry screamed and jumped back. Then he spun around and raced across the yard.

"Where are you going?!"

"A snake! A snake!"

A garter snake slithered after Larry. "*AHHHHH! AHHHHH! AHHHHH!*"

Both Larry and the snake made a circle around the yard, Larry waving his arms high in the air and shrieking. It was a good thing nobody but Max could hear him. Finally, Larry stopped running and shot up to the roof of the Zucchini Sisters' house.

The snake made a left turn and disappeared under the fence.

"It's gone, Uncle Larry!"

"Are you sure?"

"I'm sure."

Larry floated down to the patio, then sat on a deck chair. "I think I'll stay here awhile. You go ahead, Max."

Max made his way to the vegetable garden.

In the spot where the giant zucchini had grown, there was a huge indentation in the soil. Max noticed some outdoor speakers that the Puccini music must have come out of. He also noticed that the huge zucchini leaves were bent to the right. He remembered thinking Mr. Leonard was exaggerating when he said that just yesterday they had been ten feet tall. Now he could see that they probably *would be* ten feet tall if they weren't leaning over. He scanned the rest of the garden and noticed something interesting: the plants that were growing around the zucchini were bent over, too — in the same direction.

Max moved closer and bent down to examine the plants more carefully. Someone — or something — had pushed them down.

Max stood up.

He looked out over the yard, taking in the large indentation the zucchini had left;

the giant, bent-over zucchini leaves; the bent-over plants and the tiny holes in the grass. And just then, he noticed the poison ivy that had grown through the fence from Mr. Leonard's garden.

"I know who stole the zucchini," he said to himself.

CHAPTER 9

MAX SOLVES THE CASE

Max needed all the suspects in one place, so he asked the Zucchini Sisters to invite Mr. Leonard, Mr. Jordan and Edwena Whacker to join them in their garden for lemonade. When everyone had arrived, Larry looked around carefully to make sure there were no snakes, and then joined the group.

The sisters poured glasses of lemonade and handed them out, then mentioned that

Max was helping them find their stolen zucchini.

Edwena looked surprised. "Your zucchini was *stolen?*"

Zeeta and Zelda nodded gravely. "The one we were entering in the Harvest Fair."

"After all your hard work! How dreadful. Who would do such a thing?"

"One of *these* guys," said Larry, jerking his thumb at Mr. Jordan and Mr. Leonard.

"We don't know," said Zeeta. "That's why Max is here. He's a very smart young detective."

"Go on, Max," said Zelda. "Tell us what you've discovered."

"I've examined all the clues," said Max, "and I know who stole the zucchini."

Mr. Leonard, Edwena and Mr. Jordan eyeballed each other.

Max walked to the vegetable garden, where the zucchini had been lying. "The stolen zucchini grew here and weighed about two hundred pounds. A zucchini that size would be way too big and too heavy for one person to carry alone."

Larry's eyes brightened. "Whoever took it had an accomplice!" He moved closer to Max. "I'll bet Jordan and Fur Hat were working together!"

SHE'S WEARING OVEN MITTS!

Max stepped out of the garden. "Other than through the back door of the house, there's only one way into this yard, and that's through the side gate. I checked, and there aren't any fingerprints on the gate latch. That could mean the person who stole the zucchini wore gloves—"

"She's wearing oven mitts!" said Mr. Leonard, pointing at Edwena.

Everyone turned to look at Edwena.

"I've broken out in hives!" Edwena cried. "When I get nervous, I break out! Tell them, Zelda!"

"It's true," said Zelda. "Edwena's always borrowing calamine lotion to put on her hands, her face, her feet — wherever she happens to break out. She is always running out of it."

"Edwena was on my list of suspects because it would take an awful lot of zucchini to fill an order as big as she is expecting from the bakery contract. She told me herself that she didn't go to the parade. And with two brothers as strong as hers, there's no question she could have stolen the zucchini while Zeeta and Zelda were in town. But she didn't do it."

"I *knew* it wasn't her," Larry said smugly.

Max turned to face Mr. Leonard. "Mr. Leonard, you had good reason to want to get back at the sisters for ruining your tomato crop. The leaves from their zucchini blocked the sun, so your vegetables weren't given a chance to grow. But there's no evidence that you had anything to do with it, either."

Zeeta and Zelda looked shocked and sorry. "Oh, Mr. Leonard," said Zelda. "Why didn't you say something?"

Mr. Leonard shrugged.

Max turned to Mr. Jordan.

MAY I BORROW YOUR CANE?

"Mr. Jordan, I was told you *always* put gloves on before touching anything."

"It's not a secret. Everyone knows how I feel about germs. I don't see what that has to do with anything."

"The reason I mention it," said Max, "is that if you opened the gate with your gloves on, there would be no fingerprints."

Mr. Jordan sniffed. "And what does that prove?"

"Nothing — on its own."

Max bent down and pointed to the grass. "If you look carefully, you'll notice a straight row of small holes leading directly from the gate over to the zucchini." Max looked at Mr. Jordan again. "May I borrow your cane, please?"

Mr. Jordan cleared his throat and slowly handed over his cane. Max placed the bottom of the cane directly into one of the holes.

Zeeta and Zelda gasped.

"A perfect fit!" said Mr. Leonard.

"Don't be ridiculous," snapped Mr. Jordan. He yanked his cane out of Max's hand. "If you think I could lift a zucchini *that* size, you're all insane."

WHAT AM I, CHOPPED LIVER?

"That's a good point," said Max. "But there's more." Mr. Jordan frowned deeply. "All the plants around the zucchini are bent over."

Everyone's eyes went over to the plants.

"A strong wind or hard rain could have bent them —" said Max.

"But it's been sunny all week," said Zelda.

"You're right. It wasn't the weather that bent them over. It was something *else* that created the strong wind."

"Whatever could it be?" asked Zeeta.

Max looked directly at Mr. Jordan. "Twirling helicopter blades."

Larry let out a whistle. "That's brilliant, Max!"

"It's common knowledge that helicopters airlift people and animals and other large things with ropes and harnesses. You had your pilot fly over the sisters' backyard and lower a rope. Then you fastened the harness around the zucchini and off it went."

Everyone stared at Mr. Jordan. The sisters looked stunned.

"I *never* would have guessed it could be you," said Zeeta.

Mr. Jordan's face turned hard. "I'm calling my lawyer." He spun around and limped out of the yard.

"Don't let the gate hit you on your way out," said Zelda, smiling sweetly. Then she threw her arms around Max. "You did it, Max!"

Zeeta stepped up and threw her arms around both of them.

"Hey!" said Larry, sulking. "What am I, chopped liver?"

Max held out an arm, inviting Larry to join in the group hug.

Larry leaned in and grinned. "Monroe's the name — solving crimes is our game."

WELL DONE, BOYS

The following day, Edwena's brothers used their truck to pick up the Zucchini Sisters' zucchini. Mr. Jordan had stashed it in a cold storage unit.

Grandpa Harry, Larry and Max popped some popcorn, then sat in front of their television set and watched the local news cover the Harvest Fair events. Zeeta and Zelda entered their zucchini in the competition and — for the tenth straight year — they won the blue ribbon!

Harry, Larry and Max cheered.

"Well done, boys," said Harry. "Another case solved by the Monroe Detective Agency!"

SPOT THE DIFFERENCE

Detectives have to be observant.
Can you find five differences between these
two pictures?

1. Larry's tie is missing.
2. One side of Harry's mustache is missing.
3. The frog's eyes are missing.
4. Max's T-shirt is gray.
5. Harry's shoes are white.

DON'T MISS CASE #3 ...

the
GHOST
and
MAX MONROE

CASE #3
THE DIRTY TRICK

Max looked at the note. It read, Beware ... a dirty trick!
"It looks like someone's trying to warn you."
*"Yes, but who?" said Rhonda. "And what kind of dirty trick
do they mean?"*

The Mystery Hall of Fame is holding a special competition
to choose its newest member. Max's favorite author, Rhonda
Remington, is competing for a spot. But someone is trying
to ruin her chances. When Rhonda receives a warning
note that a trick is going to be played on her, she turns to
the Monroe Detective Agency. Can Max and Uncle Larry
find out who's behind the dirty trick before it's too late?

The Ghost and Max Monroe series continues with
another hilarious, fast-paced mystery, featuring a sharp
ten-year-old detective and his frightfully funny sidekick.

**The Ghost and Max Monroe
Case #3: The Dirty Trick**

L. M. Falcone

HC 978-1-77138-155-0
$12.95 US • $12.95 CDN

PB 978-1-77138-019-5
$6.95 US • $6.95 CDN

PRAISE FOR CASE #1 ...

"A ghostly (but not scary) new chapter-book mystery series kicks off ... Falcone keeps readers guessing and pages turning with humorous dialogue and a quickly paced plot." — *Kirkus Reviews*

"This beginning chapter book will engage youngsters who like mysteries mixed with silly characters." — *School Library Journal*

The Ghost and Max Monroe
Case #1: The Magic Box

L. M. Falcone

HC 978-1-77138-153-6
$12.95 US • $12.95 CDN

PB 978-1-77138-017-1
$6.95 US • $6.95 CDN